GROWLTIGER'S LAST STAND

The illustrations are
for Frederika with love

GROWLTIGER'S LAST STAND

with THE PEKES AND THE POLLICLES
and THE SONG OF THE JELLICLES

by T. S. Eliot
with pictures by Errol Le Cain

GROWLTIGER'S LAST STAND

GROWLTIGER was a Bravo Cat, who travelled on a barge:
In fact he was the roughest cat that ever roamed at large.
From Gravesend up to Oxford he pursued his evil aims,
Rejoicing in his title of 'The Terror of the Thames'.

His manners and appearance did not calculate to please;
His coat was torn and seedy, he was baggy at the knees;
One ear was somewhat missing, no need to tell you why,
And he scowled upon a hostile world from one forbidding eye.

The cottagers of Rotherhithe knew something of his fame;
At Hammersmith and Putney people shuddered at his name.
They would fortify the hen-house, lock up the silly goose,
When the rumour ran along the shore: GROWLTIGER'S ON
   THE LOOSE!

Woe to the weak canary, that fluttered from its cage;
Woe to the pampered Pekinese, that faced Growltiger's rage;
Woe to the bristly Bandicoot, that lurks on foreign ships,
And woe to any Cat with whom Growltiger came to grips!

But most to Cats of foreign race his hatred had been vowed;
To Cats of foreign name and race no quarter was allowed.
The Persian and the Siamese regarded him with fear—
Because it was a Siamese had mauled his missing ear.

Now on a peaceful summer night, all nature seemed at play,
The tender moon was shining bright, the barge at Molesey lay.
All in the balmy moonlight it lay rocking on the tide—
And Growltiger was disposed to show his sentimental side.

His bucko mate, GRUMBUSKIN, long since had disappeared,
For to the Bell at Hampton he had gone to wet his beard;
And his bosun, TUMBLEBRUTUS, he too had stol'n away –
In the yard behind the Lion he was prowling for his prey.

In the forepeak of the vessel Growltiger sate alone,
Concentrating his attention on the Lady GRIDDLEBONE.
And his raffish crew were sleeping in their barrels and their bunks –
As the Siamese came creeping in their sampans and their junks.

Growltiger had no eye or ear for aught but Griddlebone,
And the Lady seemed enraptured by his manly baritone,
Disposed to relaxation, and awaiting no surprise –
But the moonlight shone reflected from a thousand bright blue eyes.

And closer still and closer the sampans circled round,
And yet from all the enemy there was not heard a sound.
The lovers sang their last duet, in danger of their lives –
For the foe was armed with toasting forks and cruel carving knives.

Then GILBERT gave the signal to his fierce Mongolian horde;
With a frightful burst of fireworks the Chinks they swarmed aboard.
Abandoning their sampans, and their pullaways and junks,
They battened down the hatches on the crew within their bunks.

Then Griddlebone she gave a screech, for she was badly skeered;
I am sorry to admit it, but she quickly disappeared.
She probably escaped with ease, I'm sure she was not drowned –
But a serried ring of flashing steel Growltiger did surround.

The ruthless foe pressed forward, in stubborn rank on rank;
Growltiger to his vast surprise was forced to walk the plank.
He who a hundred victims had driven to that drop,
At the end of all his crimes was forced to go ker-flip, ker-flop.

Oh there was joy in Wapping when the news flew through the land;
At Maidenhead and Henley there was dancing on the strand.
Rats were roasted whole at Brentford, and at Victoria Dock,
And a day of celebration was commanded in Bangkok.

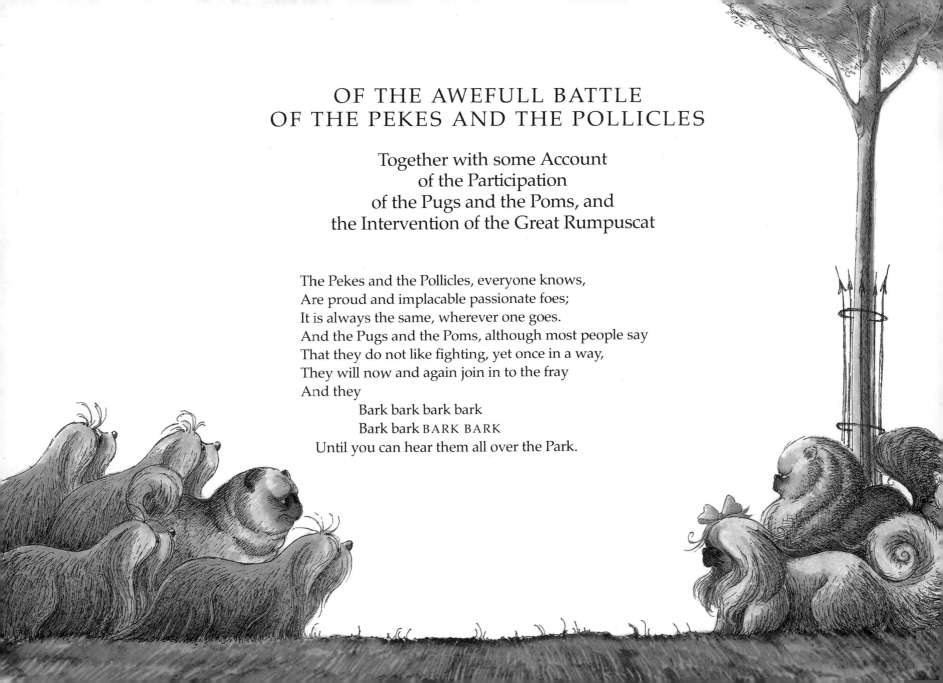

OF THE AWEFULL BATTLE
OF THE PEKES AND THE POLLICLES

Together with some Account
of the Participation
of the Pugs and the Poms, and
the Intervention of the Great Rumpuscat

The Pekes and the Pollicles, everyone knows,
Are proud and implacable passionate foes;
It is always the same, wherever one goes.
And the Pugs and the Poms, although most people say
That they do not like fighting, yet once in a way,
They will now and again join in to the fray
And they
      Bark bark bark bark
      Bark bark BARK BARK
Until you can hear them all over the Park.

Now on the occasion of which I shall speak
Almost nothing had happened for nearly a week
(And that's a long time for a Pol or a Peke).
The big Police Dog was away from his beat—
I don't know the reason, but most people think
He'd slipped into the Wellington Arms for a drink—
And no one at all was about on the street
When a Peke and a Pollicle happened to meet.

They did not advance, or exactly retreat,
But they glared at each other, and scraped their hind feet,
And started to
      Bark bark bark bark
      Bark bark BARK BARK
Until you could hear them all over the Park.

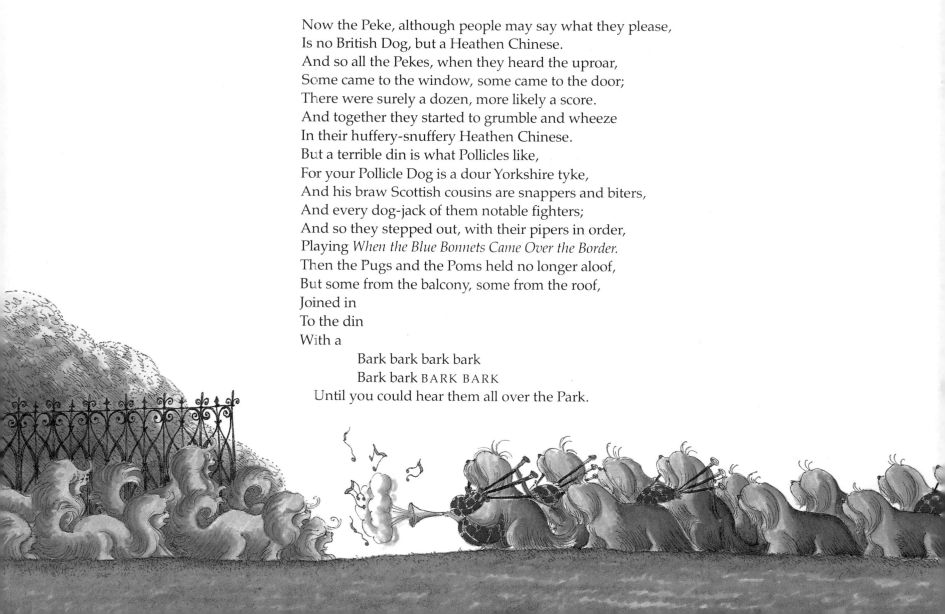

Now the Peke, although people may say what they please,
Is no British Dog, but a Heathen Chinese.
And so all the Pekes, when they heard the uproar,
Some came to the window, some came to the door;
There were surely a dozen, more likely a score.
And together they started to grumble and wheeze
In their huffery-snuffery Heathen Chinese.
But a terrible din is what Pollicles like,
For your Pollicle Dog is a dour Yorkshire tyke,
And his braw Scottish cousins are snappers and biters,
And every dog-jack of them notable fighters;
And so they stepped out, with their pipers in order,
Playing *When the Blue Bonnets Came Over the Border*.
Then the Pugs and the Poms held no longer aloof,
But some from the balcony, some from the roof,
Joined in
To the din
With a

      Bark bark bark bark
      Bark bark BARK BARK
  Until you could hear them all over the Park.

Now when these bold heroes together assembled,
The traffic all stopped, and the Underground trembled,
And some of the neighbours were so much afraid
That they started to ring up the Fire Brigade.
When suddenly, up from a small basement flat,
Why who should stalk out but the GREAT RUMPUSCAT.
His eyes were like fireballs fearfully blazing,
He gave a great yawn, and his jaws were amazing;
And when he looked out through the bars of the area,
You never saw anything fiercer or hairier.
And what with the glare of his eyes and his yawning,
The Pekes and the Pollicles quickly took warning.
He looked at the sky and he gave a great leap—
And they every last one of them scattered like sheep.

And when the Police Dog returned to his beat,
There wasn't a single one left in the street.

THE SONG OF THE JELLICLES

Jellicle Cats come out to-night,
Jellicle Cats come one come all:
The Jellicle Moon is shining bright —
Jellicles come to the Jellicle Ball.

Jellicle Cats are black and white,
Jellicle Cats are rather small;
Jellicle Cats are merry and bright,
And pleasant to hear when they caterwaul.
Jellicle Cats have cheerful faces,
Jellicle Cats have bright black eyes;
They like to practise their airs and graces
And wait for the Jellicle Moon to rise.

Jellicle Cats develop slowly,
Jellicle Cats are not too big;
Jellicle Cats are roly-poly,
They know how to dance a gavotte and a jig.
Until the Jellicle Moon appears
They make their toilette and take their repose:
Jellicles wash behind their ears,
Jellicles dry between their toes.

Jellicle Cats are white and black,
Jellicle Cats are of moderate size;
Jellicles jump like a jumping-jack,
Jellicle Cats have moonlit eyes.

They're quiet enough in the morning hours,
They're quiet enough in the afternoon,
Reserving their terpsichorean powers
To dance by the light of the Jellicle Moon.

Jellicle Cats are black and white,
Jellicle Cats (as I said) are small;
If it happens to be a stormy night
They will practise a caper or two in the hall.
If it happens the sun is shining bright
You would say they had nothing to do at all:
They are resting and saving themselves to be right
For the Jellicle Moon and the Jellicle Ball.

First published in 1986 by Faber and Faber Limited
3 Queen Square London WC1N 3AU
Printed in Great Britain by
W. S. Cowell Ltd, Ipswich

British Library Cataloguing in Publication Data

Eliot, T. S.
Growltiger's last stand.
I. Title   II. Le Cain, Errol
821'.912   PS3509.L43
ISBN 0-571-13882-9